socks

socks

BEVERLY CLEARY

illustrated by Beatrice Darwin

A YEARLING BOOK

Published by
Dell Publishing Co., Inc.
1 Dag Hammarskjold Plaza
New York, New York 10017

Yearling ® TM 913705, Dell Publishing Co., Inc.

ISBN: 0-440-48256-9

Reprinted by arrangement with William Morrow & Company, Inc.

Printed in the United States of America

May 1980

20 19 18 17 16

CW

Contents

socks

one
The Kitten Sale

The tabby kitten hooked his white paws over the edge of the box marked, *Kittens 25¢ or Best Offer*. The girl with the stringy hair and sunburned arms picked him up and set him down in the midst of his wiggling, crawling, mewing brothers and sisters. He wanted to get out; she wanted him to stay in. The puzzling struggle had gone on all morning in the space between the mailbox and the newspaper rack near the door of the supermarket.

"Nice fresh kittens for sale," called out the girl, whose name was Debbie. She usually held the kitten in her arms, and he expected her to hold him now.

"Stupid," said her brother George, embarrassed to be selling kittens with his younger sister on a summer morning. "Whoever heard of fresh kittens?"

"Me," said Debbie, as she pushed the kitten down once more. Then she repeated at the top of her voice, "Nice fresh kittens for sale." She knew she was not stupid, and she enjoyed annoying her brother. The two had quarreled at breakfast. George said Debbie should sell the kittens, because she played with them and that made them hers. Debbie said George should sell the kittens, because she didn't know how to make change. Besides, he was the one who had brought the mother home when she was a kitten, so that made her kittens his. Their father said, "Stop bickering, you two. You can *both* sell them," and that was that.

The white-pawed kitten, unaware of the hard feelings between brother and sister, tried again. He stepped on another kitten and this time managed to lift his chin over the rim of the carton. His surprised blue eyes took in a parking lot full of shoppers pushing grocery carts among cars glittering in the summer heat. He was fascinated and frightened.

"Now Socks," said Debbie, as she unhooked his claws from the cardboard, "be a good kitten."

Socks's orange-and-white sister caught his

tail and bit it. Socks rolled over on his back and swiped at her with one white paw. He no longer felt playful toward a littermate who bit his tail. Now that he was seven weeks old, he wanted to escape from all the rolling, pouncing, and nipping that went on inside the box.

Unfortunately, no shopper was willing to buy Socks his freedom. Several paused to smile at the sign, and then Socks found himself shoved to the bottom of the heap by Debbie.

"What are you going to do with all the money when you sell the kittens?" asked an elderly woman who was lonely for her grandchildren.

"Daddy says we should save up to have the mother cat shoveled, so she won't have kittens all the time," answered Debbie.

"Spayed," corrected George. "She means he said we should have the mother spayed."

"Oh, my," said the woman and hurried into the market.

"Stupid," said George. "Anyway, Dad was joking, I think."

This time Debbie looked as if she agreed with her brother that she might be stupid. "What are we going to do?" she asked, as she plucked Socks from the edge of the carton once more. "Nobody wants them."

"Mark them down, I guess. Dad said to *give* them away if we had to." The boy borrowed a felt-tipped pen from a checker in the market and, while Socks peered over the edge of the carton, crossed out the 25¢ on his sign and wrote 20¢ above it.

"Kittens for sale." Debbie's voice sounded encouraging as she hid Socks under two of his littermates. He promptly wiggled out. On a day like this his own fur was warm enough.

"Why do you keep hiding Socks?" George tried to look as if he just happened to be standing there by the mailbox and had nothing to do with the kittens.

"Because he's the best kitten, and I want to keep him," said Debbie.

"Dad won't let you," her brother reminded her. "He says the house is getting to smell like cats."

Socks found himself plucked from the litter and cradled in the girl's arms. "Well, at least we can find a good home for him." Debbie was admitting the truth of her brother's statement. "I don't want just anybody to take Socks."

"You don't see a line of people forming to buy kittens, do you?" asked George. To pass the time he had read the headlines of the newspapers in the rack and the label on the mailbox and was starting in on the signs posted in the windows of the market.

Socks tried to climb Debbie's T-shirt, but she held him back while she watched the faces of shoppers for signs of interest. Once a man approached, but he only wanted to drop a letter in the mailbox. A woman paused long enough to look at each kitten and then say, "No, I can't bear to think of anything as warm and furry as a kitten on such a hot day."

Children entering the market with their parents begged to be allowed to buy a kitten, just one, please, *please,* with their very own money, but no one actually bought a kitten. "I guess it just isn't kitten weather," said Debbie.

Socks struggled to free himself from the heat of the girl's sweaty arms. "Be good, Socks," said Debbie. "We're trying to find you a nice home."

"Fat chance." George had finished reading the signs in the window and was even more bored. Special prices on ground beef and soap and announcements of cake sales did not interest him.

A woman with her hair on rollers, wearing a muumuu and rubber-thong sandals, herded three children and a tired-looking mongrel across the parking lot. The tallest, a girl barely old enough to read, shrieked, "Mommy, look! A kitten sale!"

"I want one! I want one!" shouted her younger brother and sister.

Debbie and George exchanged a look. The dog, sensing a long argument, lay down in front of the market door where customers had to step over him. Panting used up all his energy, and he had none left with which to investigate kittens.

"I want that one with white feet," said the boy, who was wearing new swimming trunks.

"I saw him first!" The younger girl shoved her brother.

"Cut it out, you two," ordered the mother, guiding her brood across the traffic lane.

"Not Socks. *Please* not Socks." There was desperation in Debbie's whisper. Socks could feel thumping beneath her T-shirt as she held him closer. "They're the kind that will squeeze him and forget to give him water. I can tell."

George did not answer, but he frowned as the three children approached. He had good reason to quarrel with *his* sister, but that did not mean he approved of quarreling.

The oldest of the three joined the squabble. "I get him, because I'm the oldest. You two can have Bad Dog." The dog, hearing his name, lifted his head, decided nothing of importance was happening, and dropped it again.

The younger girl, who was wearing her sister's outgrown shorts and blouse, objected.

"Just because you're oldest you always think you can have everything."

"No fair!" shouted the boy. "Bad Dog belongs to all of us."

Debbie unhooked the kitten's claws from her T-shirt and tried to hide him behind her back. Socks struggled. Until this morning Debbie always had been careful to support his feet when she held him, and she never had squeezed before.

"I want that one with white feet that the girl is hiding," said the older girl.

"Me too! Me too!" The boy jumped up and down and clutched his swimming trunks, which his mother had bought for him to grow into.

"I know!" The younger sister had found a solution. "Mommy can buy us each a kitten."

"That's what you think," said the weary

mother. "One is plenty. We'll take the one with white feet."

Socks had almost wiggled free when a second pair of hands seized him. He felt himself being lifted. Metal creaked, the hands thrust him into darkness and he found himself falling. He landed on something smooth in a dark, stifling place. Above he heard a creak and a clang. Outside he heard shouting and the sound of Debbie's bursting into tears. The strangest things had happened to Socks that morning.

"He mailed him!" cried the small boy. "That big boy mailed the kitten I wanted."

"The one *I* wanted," contradicted his big sister.

"Cut it out, you kids," said the mother.

The little sister shrieked, "Mommy, he hit me!" Now she had her brother in the wrong.

Socks slipped and slid on the letters that crackled beneath his paws as he explored the dark mailbox. The place was sweltering, but it was free from other kittens. For the first time in seven weeks of life Socks had found a place where no one could step on his face or bite his tail. He lay down on the letters to catch up on the rest he had missed that morning.

Outside the commotion continued. "I'm fed up with you kids fighting all the time," said the mother. "Just for that we won't buy a kitten at all."

All three children protested. "No fair!" "You *said* you'd buy us a kitten. You promised!" "Please, Mommy. Just one. We won't fight anymore. Honest."

"Come along," said the mother, relieved to have an excuse for leaving the kitten behind. "I'll buy you popsicles. I need a kitten like a hole in the head."

This decision was followed by shouts of, "I want lime!" "I want grape!" "I don't want a popsicle! I want a Slurpy."

Socks was discovering that the heat inside the box made sleep impossible. The chute at the top opened. "Socks, are you all right down there?" Socks recognized the tearful voice as Debbie's even though it sounded loud and hollow. Then she demanded of her brother, "How are we going to get him out? He'll roast if we leave him in there. He'll starve. He'll die!" She tried to cool the box by opening and closing the creaky chute.

"You didn't want a bunch of fighting kids to get him, did you?" asked George. "You want him to go to a good home, don't you?"

"How can we sell him when he's in the mailbox?" asked Debbie. "Nobody can see him."

"Look," said George, "it says on the box that the mail will be picked up at eleven twenty-three A.M. The clock in the market says eleven fifteen. All we have to do is wait for the mailman to unlock the box and we'll get Socks back."

There was a loud sniff outside the mailbox. "Are you sure the mailman will give him back?" Hope and respect for her brother had replaced fear and anger in Debbie's voice.

"Sure, I'm sure," said George. "The post office doesn't want kittens any more than anyone else."

"I hope nobody wants to mail a package before eleven twenty-three. It might hit Socks." The tears were gone from Debbie's voice. "Nice fresh kittens for sale!" she called out, as she tried to fan air into the mailbox.

Socks stretched out panting, puzzled by all that had happened. A letter falling from above was only another puzzlement, but the heat forced him to mew in distress.

"Hang on, Socks." Debbie's voice echoed down the chute. "Help is coming."

At precisely twenty-three minutes after eleven, as he lay gasping on the letters, Socks was frightened by the sounds of keys rattling against metal. Before he could move, the side of the box dropped down and he lay blinking in the glare of the sun before an audience of shoppers.

"Well, how about that?" said the driver of the mail truck, when he saw the kitten.

"Socks!" cried Debbie, rescuing her kitten from the letters.

"Don't you know it's a Federal offense to tamper with the United States mails?" asked the driver, as he scooped mail into his sack. Debbie looked so alarmed that he said, "Relax. I'm only joking. A kitten doesn't count as mail unless he has stamps stuck on him, and even then I'm not sure."

The scene attracted more shoppers. A young couple pushing a cart of groceries toward the parking lot paused to watch what was going on. Debbie, trusting their appearance, held Socks up for their inspection. "This is Socks," she said. "We named him Socks, because he looks like he's wearing white socks."

"He's the smartest kitten in the bunch," said George, his voice brimming with hope. If they sold one kitten, they could sell more, and he would be free to go to the library.

Unaware that his future was about to be decided, Socks struggled and mewed to be put down. Debbie would not let him go. "See," she said to the young couple, "he likes you."

"Look at his little paws and his little pointy tail," cried the young woman, whose name was Marilyn Bricker. "And look at his beautiful markings: those black stripes on his head and the black rings around his tail like the rings on a raccoon's tail and those little white socks. Oh Bill, we must take him. We need a cat to sleep in front of the fireplace this winter now that we have a house."

"He's a very smart kitten." George pressed for a sale. "He's housebroken, too."

"I always wanted a kitten when I was a kid," remarked Bill Bricker, "but my mother didn't like cats."

"Then you should have a kitten now," said his wife.

Debbie and George exchanged a look that wiped away their disagreements of the morning. They were about to sell a kitten.

Mr. Bricker reached into the pocket of his jeans for change. "Fifty cents is the best offer I can make," he said with a smile.

"Oh, that's all right." Debbie was willing to

be generous. "Daddy said to give them away if we had to."

"Thank you," said George, as he accepted two twenty-five-cent pieces.

Debbie felt she should say something to make the transaction official. "Satisfaction guaranteed or your money—" She thought better of what she was about to say and instead handed the kitten to Mrs. Bricker. "Bye, Socks," she said. "Be a good kitten."

Socks found himself cuddled, not squeezed, in the arms of the strange Mrs. Bricker while George said to his sister, "Look, if you're ever going to learn to make change, you've got to learn that fifty cents is a lot more than twenty cents."

"Socks, did you hear what the girl said?" Mrs. Bricker stroked the tabby markings on the tiny head. "She said satisfaction guaran-

teed." Socks's eyes were closing. He was worn out by all that had happened that morning.

"To us or to the kitten?" asked Mr. Bricker, as he lifted the bags of groceries over the tail gate of an old station wagon.

"To the kitten, of course." Marilyn Bricker laughed affectionately. "I know you and your heart of Jello."

TWO
The Brickers' Other Pet

The Brickers drove Socks to a shabby house with a weedy lawn, a fragrant lemon bush, and geraniums growing in earth comfortable for a kitten to dig in. They made a bed for Socks from a carton and an old sweat shirt and placed it in the laundry beside his dish. They did not object when he chose instead to

sleep on the couch in the living room, which, except for a chair with loopy upholstery, was furnished in what the Brickers described to their college-student friends as "contemporary cast-off." They fed him canned and dry cat foods and bought raw meat for him. They wiped his paws on a good bath towel whenever he came in with wet feet, because they had not been married long enough to have an old bath towel, and when the winter rains came, they supplied him with a pan of Kitty Litter.

The Brickers talked to their cat. "Socks, you're getting a lot of service around here," said Mr. Bricker, as he left his studies to get down on his hands and knees and retrieve the ping-pong ball Socks had batted under the chest of drawers out of reach of his paw.

"Such silky fur." Mrs. Bricker spoke in her just-for-Socks voice as she left off typing to press her cheek against his coat and let her long hair fall over him like a curtain. Socks's throat throbbed with purrs. He was especially happy when he could interrupt her work on the papers that she typed for students. Her typewriter was his rival for her attention, and Socks did not like rivals.

The only real unpleasantness in Socks's new life was an unhappy day spent in a veterinary's hospital, which was soon forgotten. Socks thrived. His eyes changed from blue to the color of new leaves. He grew into a sleek cat, affectionate toward his loving owners but firm about getting his own way. He was the center of the Bricker household, and he was content.

Then a strange thing happened. Mrs. Bricker's lap began to shrink. One day Socks was perfectly comfortable resting on her knees, and the next day he did not have quite enough room. Each time he napped on her lap, he had to curl himself into a tighter ball with his tail wrapped more closely around his body. Finally one evening, when trying to find room to rest his chin, he lost his balance and fell to the floor with a thump. Both Brickers burst out laughing. Socks was insulted. He turned his back and twitched his tail back and forth across the carpet to show his displeasure.

"Poor Socks!" said Mrs. Bricker between giggles. "You lost your dignity, didn't you?"

"Come on, old boy!" coaxed Mr. Bricker. "Try my lap for size." He moved his chair away from his desk to make room.

The tail twitched. The Brickers would have to work harder before Socks would forgive them. Owners must be disciplined. If they really wanted to be forgiven, they would have to tempt him with a snack from the refrigerator.

Instead of going to the kitchen, Mrs. Bricker suddenly said in an urgent voice, "Bill! It's time to go."

"Are you sure?" Mr. Bricker's voice registered excitement, worry, and joy all at once.

Socks waited. These people had to learn.

"I'm positive," said Mrs. Bricker in a small, scared voice. "This is it."

With great dignity Socks stalked to the one piece of furniture forbidden him: the chair with the loopy upholstery. He placed his forepaws on the chair, arched his back, and pulled. *Rip, rip, rip*. There.

The Brickers gave Socks attention, but not in the way that he expected. He found himself snatched up, carried down the hall, and tossed into the dark laundry beside his pan of Kitty Litter. The door shut after him. "Sorry, old boy," said Mr. Bricker, as he gave the door an extra push to make sure it was latched.

After a moment of shocked silence, Socks let out a yowl of rage and waited for release. He could hear the Brickers talking in quick, anxious voices. He could hear the *whir-whir-whir* of the telephone dial, but he did not hear anyone coming down the hall to let him out.

Socks meowed his loudest, crossest meow. Footsteps hurried, the front door slammed, out on the driveway the old station wagon started, died, started again and drove away. The house was silent. So was Socks. After months of catnip and kidney, of service and attention, to be treated like this!

In the days that followed, Mr. Bricker dumped food into Socks's dish early in the morning before he left the house and again at night after he returned, but in between Socks was alone. He waited on the window-sill, he slept, he honed his claws on the forbidden chair, although the sport was gone. The ringing of the telephone made him anxious when no one was home to answer. The buzzing of the doorbell frightened him, so that he hid under the bed, but he need not have bothered now. No one came to open the door. Socks lost interest in food. His ping-pong ball no longer amused him. Without love he was bewildered and dejected.

Then late one morning Socks was roused from a doze by the slam of the station-wagon door on the driveway and the sound of the

voices of both his owners. With glad meows he sprang from the couch. As soon as the door opened, Socks was outside, his forepaws against Mrs. Bricker's thigh, stretching up to be petted. A light breeze ruffled his fur, and spring sunshine drew the fragrance from the lemon blossoms. Life was good again.

"Did you miss me, Socks?" Mrs. Bricker stooped to rub the hollow behind his ears where his fur grew short and fine. "Were you lonesome without me?" she asked.

Socks's throat pulsated with purrs. He rubbed against her legs, back and forth, round and round, as she entered the house. He could not get enough petting to satisfy his pent-up loneliness.

"I missed you, too," said Mrs. Bricker in such an understanding voice that Socks felt he must take advantage of her. With a hopeful meow, he started toward the kitchen, paused, and looked back to encourage her to follow him to the refrigerator. Until that moment he had been so happy to see his family that he had not noticed the bundle in Mr. Bricker's arms.

Socks hesitated. Which was more important, a tidbit from the refrigerator or his right to investigate everything that came into the house? Curiosity won, and he turned back.

"See what we've brought," said Mr. Bricker.

A smacking noise came from inside the bundle. Instantly Socks was alert. There was something alive in there. His spine prickled, and he paused to sniff cautiously.

Mrs. Bricker folded back the blanket, and Mr. Bricker leaned over so Socks could see. He saw a creature with a small, wrinkled, furless face, a sight that made his hair stand on end. His eyes grew large and he backed away. Whatever the thing was, he did not trust it.

As Socks stared at the strange creature in the bundle and listened to it smack and snuffle, he began to understand. His owners, his faithful, loving owners, had brought home a new pet to threaten his position in the household. Socks turned his back and lashed his swollen tail. He was filled with jealousy and anger and a terrible anxiety. The Brickers might love the new pet more than they loved him.

"Poor Socks." Mrs. Bricker stooped to smooth his fur, but Socks moved away from her hand.

An unhappy wail came from the bundle.

"Oh, dear! He can't be hungry already." The worry in Mrs. Bricker's voice was a new sound to Socks.

"He sure can," said Mr. Bricker, as he sat

down on the couch with the wailing bundle on the lap that had always belonged to Socks. "Listen to him! You can tell he has a fine pair of lungs."

Socks turned his back and began washing to pass the time until he made up his mind how to regain the lap from the new pet.

On her way to the kitchen, Mrs. Bricker spoke in her special voice, higher than her normal voice, that she always had used for her cat. "I'm hurrying," she said. "I'll have your bottle in a minute."

Socks paused in his washing with one paw behind his ear until he understood that this time she was not speaking to him, a slight that hurt him almost as much as the loss of the lap. He scrubbed his paw back and forth across his nose until he could contain his longing for reassurance no longer.

Alert and ready to run at the first sign of

danger, Socks crept cautiously toward Mr. Bricker, who reached for the bottle his wife had brought from the kitchen and said, "Let me feed him. You sit down and rest."

Mrs. Bricker sat down, but she did not rest. "Are you sure you know how to feed him?" she asked. Both parents spoke of the baby as "he," as if he were a stranger whose name they had not caught.

"Nothing to it." Mr. Bricker offered the bottle to his son. Greedy smacks came from the bundle. "Hey, look at him go!" said the proud new father.

Socks took a chance. He leaped to the center of the couch, cautiously set one paw on Mr. Bricker's knee, leaned forward, and sniffed a sweet, milky fragrance.

"Careful, Socks," warned Mr. Bricker. "You can look but don't come too close."

Socks stared at the tiny wrinkled face with

a mixture of fear, curiosity, and jealousy. He
saw the baby open his eyes and raise one night-
gown-covered fist as if he did not know it belonged to him. He saw the baby's head wobble
and his eyes cross. Socks began to understand
that the creature was not a pet but a new kind
of person, a person so small that he left room
on the lap for a cat. Very well. They would

share the lap, but this concession did not mean he liked the new person. Socks felt that half a lap was better than none.

Socks put a second paw on Mr. Bricker's knee, and with his eyes half-closed he began to knead and to purr.

"Ouch." Both of Mr. Bricker's hands were occupied. "Take your claws out of my leg."

Socks found himself lifted by Mrs. Bricker and set on the floor without so much as a kind word. He resumed his washing to show his owners that he had business of his own to take care of. Let them attend to theirs; he would attend to his. He groomed his tail with long, hard rasps of his pink tongue. The baby's smacking changed to fussing, another sound new to Socks. He hoisted his hind leg and went to work on his toes while he observed all that was going on. Beyond his hoisted leg he could see Mrs. Bricker leaning anxiously over her baby.

"Maybe he needs to be burped," she said.

Mr. Bricker held up the bottle. "You're right. He's taken two ounces." He set the bottle on the table at the end of the couch, raised the baby to his shoulder, and began to pat its back. Still the baby fussed. Mr. Bricker patted harder.

Socks lowered his leg. There was plenty of room on the lap. No, better not risk reclaiming it so soon. He went on with his grooming, but he began to grow uneasy. He wanted the fretting to stop, the same way he always wanted the ringing of the telephone or the buzzing of the doorbell to be silenced.

"Try rubbing instead of patting," suggested the anxious mother. The father rubbed. The fussing became a wail. Mr. Bricker rubbed the tiny back, and Mrs. Bricker patted. Socks became so anxious to have the crying stop that he no longer could pay attention to his washing.

"Maybe we don't pat the right way," said the mother.

"How else can you pat?" The father was beginning to see that there was more to feeding a baby than he had realized.

Socks took a chance and leaped up to fill the lap, which was going to waste.

Mrs. Bricker promptly returned him to the floor. Socks was deeply hurt. Filled with sorrow and longing, he lay down on the carpet with his chin on his white forepaw and stared into the black and empty fireplace. He yearned to be held and stroked and reassured. He longed to have his master hold him and play with his tail, and Socks was most particular about allowing people to play with his tail. With a deep sigh, Socks closed his eyes, but he did not sleep. His ears, moving like tiny radar screens, picked up every sound.

"What are we going to do?" Mrs. Bricker sounded almost tearful. "If we don't get the air bubble up, his stomach will go on hurting, and he's too little to hurt."

"Feeding a baby can't be this hard." The father no longer sounded confident. "The world is full of dumbbells who feed babies. How else do babies survive?"

"Try putting him face down across your knees," suggested Mrs. Bricker. "I saw somebody do that once."

The radar ears caught the soft sounds of the baby being moved, followed by gentle patting. "Try rubbing," suggested the hovering mother again.

Suddenly the baby belched. Startled, Socks raised his head and stared. The whole family was relieved: the baby, the mother and the father, who were beaming at the miraculous thing their baby had done. Socks was relieved, too, because at last the crying had stopped.

"Charles William!" Mrs. Bricker spoke to her accomplished son by name. "Ooh, such a big noise from such a little fellow!"

"Atta boy!" Mr. Bricker congratulated his son. "That's the old fight!"

The atmosphere of the room had changed from one of anxiety to one of joy, which Socks felt was his to share. This time he stood at Mr. Bricker's feet and looked up uncertainly as if to say, "I'm part of the family, too." The Brickers were too busy to notice.

"Why, Charles William is asleep already," whispered Mrs. Bricker, as she bent over her

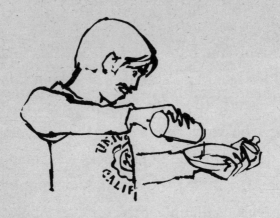

son. "Here, let me take him. I'll put him down in his crib."

Now, thought Socks. Now with the new person out of the room, he would regain the lap. Before he could jump, however, Mr. Bricker picked up the bottle, which still held several ounces of the baby's formula, and started toward the kitchen. Socks got there first and sat down beside the refrigerator. See how patiently I am waiting beside our refrigerator, his attitude seemed to say.

Mr. Bricker unscrewed the top from the bottle. "Socks, it isn't time for you to eat," he said, and was about to dump the formula into the sink when Socks uttered such a wistful meow that he changed his mind. Mr. Bricker found a bowl, poured the formula into it, and carried it into the laundry where his feet crunched through the Kitty Litter that Socks had scattered the night before. He set the bowl on the newspaper beside Socks's dish. Socks crouched and began to lap the sweet-smelling milk with his quick pink tongue.

"Did you think we had forgotten you?" asked Mr. Bricker.

Although Socks did not care to be interrupted while eating, this time he made an ex-

ception and gave his master a long stare that said, How could you bring that new person into our house? Now you have spoiled everything.

Sad and confused, Socks went back to lapping up the formula in the bowl. The warmth and sweetness of the milk comforted him. He lapped every drop and then licked the empty dish so hard that he moved it across the newspaper until it bumped the wall. Socks needed every drop of consolation he could get. His owners loved the baby more than they loved him.

THREE

Socks and the Formula

The arrival of Charles William upset the order of Socks's life. Meals were no longer served on time. Laps were always occupied. Lights were turned on in the night. The washing machine swished and the dryer hummed at odd hours. The house was filled with lint from new diapers, which tickled his nose. The

Brickers' friends, who once had admired Socks, now came to admire the baby. Tiffy, the little girl next door who loved babies and who also liked to pick up cats, usually around the middle, came to watch Charles William's bath almost every morning. Socks spent a lot of time sneezing among the fluffs of dust under the bed in the front bedroom, where Tiffy could not get at him.

The one comfort in Socks's life was leftover formula, sometimes a few drops and sometimes an ounce or two, which was poured into his bowl after the baby was fed. Socks began to wait for the sound of Charles William smacking at his bottle.

That baby! His cries grew louder and his smacks greedier. His neck became strong enough to support his head. His eyes stopped crossing. He made the exciting discovery that his hands belonged to him, and he waved them happily. He kicked his feet and said, "Ug-gug-gug."

"He's a big boy. Yes, he is!" cried Mrs. Bricker in the voice that used to belong to her cat.

Socks, on the other hand, grew lazy. Instead of chasing his ping-pong ball across the living room, down the hall, and into the bedroom, where Mr. Bricker would have to reach for it, he now patted it with a curved paw and let it roll off by itself. When the mailman brought Charles William another present, Socks examined the wrapping paper, but he no longer bothered to hide under it or to play with the ribbon.

One Sunday afternoon Socks, comfortably full of warm formula, was dozing in a patch of sunshine on the living-room carpet when another set of visitors arrived to see the baby. They were Charles William's Uncle Walter, Aunt Cassie, and eight-year-old cousin Mike, who was carrying a package wrapped in paper printed with blue rabbits. Socks remembered these people. Aunt Cassie's lap was narrow and hard. Uncle Walter enjoyed rumpling a cat's fur so that the cat had to lick and lick and lick to get himself in order. Mike teased. This afternoon, however, Socks felt too comfortable and drowsy to flee.

The first thing Uncle Walter did upon entering the house was to take off his hat, which he wore to cover his bald head, and shy it across the room so that it landed on Socks. "Hi ya, Socks, old boy," said Uncle Walter. Then he added to Mr. Bricker, his brother-in-law, "I see you're still keeping that cat."

Socks glared from under the brim of the hat, but he did not budge.

Mrs. Bricker proudly carried Charles William into the living room to show him to her brother's family. She had dressed him in one of the many little knit suits that the mailman had brought, and his rosy feet were bare.

Charles William took one look at Uncle Walter and screamed. Socks came out from under the hat with a start and retreated under a chair. He recognized fear when he heard it and accepted the scream as a warning of danger. If Charles William was in danger, so was he. Maybe Charles William was of some use after all.

Mrs. Bricker also recognized the cry of fear. She sat down on the couch and held Charles William close. "Did something frighten the baby?" she asked tenderly. "It's all right. Nothing's going to hurt the baby."

Charles William hid his face in his mother's neck and sobbed.

"Maybe a pin is sticking him," suggested Uncle Walter.

Charles William, braver when his mother held him close, stole a look at the visitors, shrieked again, and shivering with sobs hid his face. Socks peered from under the chair. Everyone was seated, and although the Brickers were concerned, no one appeared frightened.

"Oh, it's just Walter's bald head," said Aunt Cassie matter-of-factly. "All babies are frightened the first time they see a bald head."

"What am I supposed to do?" asked Uncle Walter. "Take off my head and carry it under my arm?"

Aunt Cassie, not a woman for baby talk, took hold of Charles William's hand. "Charles William, you are a fine healthy boy," she said, and turned to her son. "Mike, say hello to your new cousin."

"Hi, Chuckie," said Mike, who plainly thought babies boring. Visiting relatives was boring, too, and a waste of a good afternoon. He set the package on the couch as if he were glad to be rid of it and flopped back into a chair.

Charles William took his face out of his mother's neck, looked at Uncle Walter, and howled again.

"For goodness' sake, Walter, put on your hat," said Aunt Cassie. "Nobody cares if you wear it in the house, and you can't expect a baby to understand the whole world all at once."

Uncle Walter picked up his hat from the carpet and did as he was told. Charles William's sobs ceased.

With the danger, whatever it was, out of the way, Socks turned a wary eye on Mike, who was slumped in a chair staring at the ceiling.

The boy looked harmless enough, but Socks did not trust him for a minute. As he watched, his ears picked up the faint threatening wail of another cat, the sort of wail that leads to fighting with fangs and claws. The wail grew louder. Where could the cat be? Socks looked anxiously around the room, half expecting to see the old black cat that sometimes prowled across the backyard. The sound was all the more frightening because Socks could not find the creature who was making it.

"Mike, stop that noise," said Aunt Cassie. "You'll frighten Charles William. And stop slouching."

The cat wail stopped, but Socks continued to keep an eye out for the enemy. He also watched Mike, who remained slumped in the chair, bored with the opening of the gift, bored with all the exclamations over the brown cor-

duroy bear that his mother had bought at a church bazaar.

The small bear caught Socks's attention, and he did not find it boring at all. The bear was going to make a good sparring partner, and Socks could not wait to get at it.

"All babies love soft bears, and I knew you had enough clothes by now," said Aunt Cassie, who was holding Charles William on her lap. "Have you started him on egg yolk yet?"

Socks looked longingly at the bear, which Mrs. Bricker was holding on her lap as if she needed something to take the place of Charles William.

"Say, Bill," said Uncle Walter to Mr. Bricker, "have you thought about buying the kid an encyclopedia? Now's a good time. The price goes up the first of the year."

Mr. Bricker tried to swallow a yawn. He had given Charles William his bottle at two o'clock that morning, and getting the air bubble out of him had taken longer than usual.

Mike was bored with the egg-yolk discussion. He was bored with his father, sitting there under his hat, trying to sell a set of encyclopedia. He stared thoughtfully at Socks, who was still watching the bear from under the chair. Then, looking innocently in another direction, Mike parted his lips and began to pant in short, quick pants like a dog.

The pupils of Socks's golden-green eyes grew large and black. A dog in the house? Where?

The enemy cat returned with a threatening wail. The dog panted. Socks was terrified. He was surrounded by invisible enemies. Wild-eyed, he darted from under the chair to the center of the rug.

Panting harder, the invisible dog seemed to be coming closer.

"Say, hasn't that cat put on a lot of weight?" asked Uncle Walter, who had been forced to admit that Charles William would not be ready to read for a few years, and by then the encyclopedia might be out of date.

"You know," said Aunt Cassie, who was

letting Charles William clutch her finger, "overweight animals are subject to heart trouble the same as overweight people." Her voice then shifted to a higher note. "Does the baby see the kitty? Look at the fat kitty."

"You're right. He *is* gaining weight." Mrs. Bricker sounded surprised, as if she had not taken time to look at her cat lately.

Charles William, turning his head in the direction of the cat-fight sound, looked worried. Socks decided to risk the run to the safety of the bedroom, but Uncle Walter reached out and caught him as he tried to go by. Socks struggled. Uncle Walter would not let him go.

"Mike, I told you to stop that!" said Aunt Cassie, and continued with her discussion of Socks's weight problem. "That cat should be put on a diet before it's too late. Our poor old

Lassie is much healthier now that we have her on a salt-free, low-cholesterol diet."

"The dog gets chicken breasts; we get hamburgers," said Uncle Walter, amusing himself by rumpling the cat's fur.

"I buy chicken breasts on sale and freeze them." Aunt Cassie had an answer for everything.

Socks endured the rumpling the best he could, but the minute the big hands released him, he crouched close to the floor and glared in pure hatred at Uncle Walter. Then, looking anxiously from right to left and back again, he fled from the living room to his hideaway under the bed. There he remained among the dust fluffs, sneezing occasionally and trying to put his fur in order in a space so low that he could not sit up. Everything was wrong. He hated Uncle Walter and distrusted Mike. Aunt

Cassie did not admire him. Worn out by the events of the afternoon and with his fur in disarray, Socks fell asleep. Things were sure to be better at suppertime.

Even though Socks slept, his radar ears told him what was going on. The visitors departed. Charles William took his bottle. When the ears relayed the second burp to Socks's brain, he came out from under the bed and, trailing dust from his whiskers, ran down the hall to the kitchen in time to meet Mr. Bricker with the formula bottle.

"Sorry, Socks," said Mr. Bricker, unscrewing the cap. "Cassie is right. You're too fat."

Socks looked up and meowed to tell his master how hungry he was and how much in need of comfort after a terrible afternoon.

"Beat it." Mr. Bricker's words were rude, but his voice was kindly. "We can't have any fat cats around this house. We keep fit around here."

Mrs. Bricker entered the kitchen to prepare supper. "I'm going to watch my diet, too," she said, as her husband dumped Socks's share of the warm milk down the drain. "And I'm going to start exercising. I still can't zip all my slacks." She raised her arms and bent to touch her toes.

Socks was outraged. What was the matter with these people? He was supposed to have formula now. He always had formula after Charles William. These people could not treat him this way. He placed his front paws on Mr. Bricker's leg and meowed to let his feelings be known.

"Sorry." Mr. Bricker had made up his mind to start Socks on a program of physical fitness.

"One, two, one, two." Mrs. Bricker continued to touch her toes.

Socks unsheathed his claws the least bit and let them prick Mr. Bricker's leg.

"Ouch. Cut that out." Mr. Bricker unhooked the claws and walked out of the kitchen, leaving Socks to sulk beside the refrigerator while Mrs. Bricker, out of breath from her exercise, prepared the evening meal.

"All right, Socks," she finally said, after she had tripped over him twice and stepped on his tail, "I'll feed you now and get you out of the way." She laid four pieces of kidney instead of eight on the dish in the laundry room. Socks gulped them down and looked up as if to say, "Where's the rest of my meal?" Four pieces of meat would not get him out of the way when he was used to eight.

"Silly cat," said Mrs. Bricker with affec-

tion. "You and I are going to lose weight."
Socks sat down beside the refrigerator and
gave his whiskers a quick swipe with his paw
while he thought the problem over.

When Charles William fussed in the back
bedroom, and Mrs. Bricker hurried off to attend to him, Socks saw his chance. He sprang
to the counter where he was disappointed to
discover that the Brickers were having wien-
ers for supper. Too hungry to be choosy, he
sank his teeth into a link and thumped to the
floor.

"Socks!" shouted Mrs. Bricker, who heard
the thump and knew its meaning.

Socks ran in a guilty crouch through the
laundry and down the hall to his refuge under the bed. Mr. Bricker was after him with
the broom. "We can't let you get away with
that," he said on his hands and knees, as he

lifted the Indian bedspread and poked at his cat. "Come on out of there."

Socks carried his prey to the farthest corner against the wall and, growling, faced Mr. Bricker. This was his wiener, and he was willing to fight for it. Mr. Bricker pushed the broom at him, but Socks did not budge. He growled more fiercely and his fur rose along his spine. Let his owner yell and poke. He was hungry, and he was going to have that wiener.

The broom jabbed again. Socks dropped his wiener in the dust and, with every hair standing on end, hissed.

Mr. Bricker laughed. "Okay, you win this time, but next time, look out!" He rose to his knees and left Socks to his prey.

Socks settled down to gnaw the wiener as fiercely as if he had stalked and killed it. If his owners did not care enough about him to feed him properly, he would live by his wits.

FOUR

The Evening the Sitter Came

Mr. Bricker sang while he changed Charles William's diaper. "Feed the baby garlic, so we'll find him in the dark. Oh, a boy's best friend is his mother."

"There's a little wheel a-turning in my heart," sang Mrs. Bricker, as she folded diapers. Life was easier for the young parents.

Charles William, who now ate egg yolk, vegetables, and strained meat, could sleep through the night without a bottle at two o'clock in the morning.

Socks, not so fortunate, still woke up at two o'clock expecting formula to be poured into his bowl. He felt cheated by the diet meals that his owners served him. After his small nutritious breakfast, he was allowed to sit beside the refrigerator all day without an offer of a bite to eat. He waited for food to be left on the counter so he could steal it, but his owners were too smart for him. Socks was reduced to catching and eating moths.

The Brickers not only refused to give Socks all he wanted to eat, they insisted that he exercise. Mr. Bricker tied a wad of cellophane to the end of a string and dragged it around the carpet for Socks to chase. "Come on, cat," he said. "You still have some fat to work off." After a few turns around the room, Socks, breathing heavily, found lying down easier than playing.

The empty feeling in his middle sharpened Socks's hunting instincts. He stalked Mrs. Bricker's furry bedroom slippers until she caught him and shut them away in the closet. He crouched, waggled his rump, and pounced on the brown corduroy bear when Charles

William shoved it out of his crib. He carried it around in his mouth until Charles William set up such a howl that Mrs. Bricker rescued the bear and returned it to its owner.

"Bad Socks," she scolded. "You leave Brown Bear alone."

Socks gave her a cold look. Couldn't she see he was not bad? He was hungry.

Late afternoons were hardest for Socks, for then Mrs. Bricker sat on the couch holding Charles William, draped in a diaper to catch spills, and spooned cereal, strained meat, vegetables, and applesauce from custard cups into his messy mouth. "See the kitty," she said, as Socks watched hungrily. "See the fat kitty."

The fat kitty did not care about cereal, vegetables, and applesauce, but he resented the baby's getting that meat. However, he

knew how to get even. He walked to the front
door and meowed.

Socks now had Mrs. Bricker at a disadvan-
tage. Both her hands and her lap were occupied, and she did not know whether her
cat merely *wanted* to go out or whether he
needed to. Socks meowed a second time.

"Oh, Socks," said Mrs. Bricker with a sigh.
"Do you have to?"

Socks meowed a third time, and as he knew
she would, Mrs. Bricker set the custard cup
she was holding on the coffee table, carried
Charles William, who fussed at the interrup-
tion, across the room, and opened the door.
"Socks, we love you," she said, "but you are
getting to be a nuisance. A big fat nuisance."
When Socks took his time walking through
the door, she gave his tail a little push with
her toe and shut the door behind him.

Socks was determined to satisfy the empty feeling in his middle. He leaped the fence and meowed pitifully at the neighbor's back door, because the back door was closest to the refrigerator. When the elderly woman who lived there opened the door, Socks lifted his nose and breathed in the fragrance of stew simmering on the stove. Mrs. Bricker had not cooked anything that smelled this good since Charles William had arrived.

"Now Socks, you old fraud, don't you come begging around here." The neighbor was kind, but she meant what she said. "You can't tell me you haven't had anything to eat, because I know better." As she spoke she tossed a handful of peanuts onto the grass for the blue jays that came swooping down from the television aerial.

Socks hated jays, noisy yammering birds

that dived at him every chance they got. While the jays were busy picking up peanuts and storing them under the shingles of the Brickers' roof, Socks sneaked across his own yard to the house on the other side.

Unfortunately, Tiffy opened the door to his meow, but Socks took a chance and rubbed against her legs. Charm was often helpful.

"Mommy, Socks likes me!" shrieked Tiffy.

"Lucky you," answered her mother from another room.

Socks tactfully led the way to the refrigerator. "Mommy, Socks is hungry!" Tiffy called out.

"Don't let that cat kid you," her mother called back.

"Can I feed him?"

"Sure. Go ahead," said Tiffy's mother.

Juices ran in Socks's mouth as Tiffy pulled open the white door. She took out a plastic pitcher, poured something in a cup, and set it on the floor. "There you are, Socksie," she said tenderly. "Nice Hawaiian punch."

One whiff was enough. Socks gave Tiffy a look of reproach. How could she disappoint him like this?

Tiffy squatted beside him. "Try it, Socksie. You'll like it," she coaxed. "How do you know you won't like it if you don't try it?"

Socks's answer was a long look at the refrigerator. Tiffy got the idea. This time she offered him leftover chocolate pudding, which he also disdained. Obviously this household had nothing fit for a cat to eat. He walked to the back door and asked to go out. These people were not worth bothering with. Tiffy, eager to do something to please

the cat, opened the door. "Bye, Socksie," she said in a voice sad with disappointment. Socks walked out with his tail erect and quirked at the tip like a question mark.

Where could Socks beg next? Cars and dogs made the territory in front of the house dangerous. The evil jays, having hidden their peanuts, were now finding them and rapping them on the roof to crack them. The sight of the jowly black cat sunning himself on the back fence was discouraging.

Socks slunk home and let himself in through an open window. As his paws hit the floor there came a sound he had not heard since the arrival of Charles William, the sound of Mrs. Bricker tapping down the hall in her going-out-for-the-evening shoes. Instantly he was alert for the answers to two important questions. Would he be fed before his owners left, and would he be shut inside or outside the house?

"*Prreow*." Socks half purred and half meowed as he rubbed against the legs of Mr. Bricker, who was sitting on the bed tying his shoes. Mr. Bricker responded by rubbing his cat's head roughly and affectionately, but he made no move in the direction of the refrigerator.

Mrs. Bricker tapped down the hall into the bedroom with Charles William in her arms. "Is our big boy going to miss his mommy and daddy?" she asked.

"*Prreow*," begged Socks at his most charming. "*Prreow*."

"Yes," said Mrs. Bricker. "The kitty's talking to the baby." She was wrong. Socks was not talking to the baby. He never talked to the baby.

"Do you think Charles William will mind our going out?" the young mother asked anxiously, as Charles William grabbed a handful of her long hair. "He's beginning to understand so many things."

"If he does mind, he'll have to get used to the idea," said Mr. Bricker. "Mom said we were to spend the check she sent on a baby sitter and an evening out. You need to get out once in a while, and the world is full of babies who have survived an evening with a sitter."

"*Prreow.*" A cat needed attention, too.

"All right, Socks, you old beggar," said Mr. Bricker. "Let's feed you and get you out of the way."

Socks's victory was small—four pieces of meat—and while he was gulping them, the doorbell rang. The sound always unsettled him, but curiosity forced him to investigate.

Mrs. Bricker opened the front door to a plump elderly woman, who was carrying a paper shopping bag and who introduced herself. "I am Mrs. Risley from the Sitters' Service Agency." She entered and leaned her shopping bag against the chair with the loopy upholstery. "Hello there, young man," she said to Charles William, as she removed her coat and, without waiting to be asked, hung it in the closet beside the front door.

Socks sniffed at the shopping bag, which had a tantalizing smell. He stood on his hind legs with his front paws against the chair and peered into the bag, but all he could see were some yarn and knitting needles. He dropped to all fours and sniffed again. Interesting!

"Well, hello, you old Skeezix!" All cats were Skeezix to Mrs. Risley, who stooped to rub Socks behind his ears. "My, aren't you a big handsome boy with a nice thick coat!"

Socks sat down and looked up at Mrs. Risley with love in his eyes. Here at last was a true admirer, his first since the baby had arrived.

"Charles William has had his supper," said Mrs. Bricker, who had not trusted a stranger to feed her baby, "but he will want a bottle when he goes down for the night. He's big enough to hold his own bottle now, and he doesn't need to be burped anymore."

"And what about Skeezix?" asked Mrs. Risley. "What do I feed him?"

"He's been fed," answered Mrs. Bricker with her eyes on her son. "And don't let him tell you he hasn't. He's quite a beggar, but for a while he was getting too fat. For your supper there is—"

"Oh, don't worry about me," said Mrs. Risley. "I always bring a meat patty with me. On these jobs you never know what you're going to find to eat. Some places all you get is a can of soup or a waffle." She reached for Charles William, who looked surprised and uncertain. He turned to his mother for some explanation and whimpered.

"He's going to be all right." Mr. Bricker firmly guided his wife to the door.

Charles William began to cry, and Socks stopped his investigation of the shopping bag. He looked anxiously at the three adults, wanting them to attend to the baby.

"Don't you worry about a thing," said Mrs. Risley. "He'll stop crying as soon as you leave. They always do."

Mrs. Risley was right. As soon as his parents disappeared, Charles William discovered the scarf below Mrs. Risley's double chin and stopped crying. He had never seen a scarf like hers before and found it interesting. "Eh-yeh-yeh," he said.

"That's better," said Mrs. Risley, and sat Charles William in his playpen. She began to rummage in her shopping bag. "I call this my survival kit," she said to Socks, who was peering into the bag to see if she had something for him. From the jumble of knitting, crayons, scissors, colored paper, magazines, and bedroom slippers, Mrs. Risley produced a roll of Scotch tape and, tearing off a piece, stuck it firmly to the big toe of Charles William's bare left foot. "There," she said. "That will keep you busy." Once again she was right.

Charles William stared at his toe in astonishment. Never before had he experienced Scotch tape on his toe. He lay back and waved his foot. The tape stuck fast. Fascinating! "Ah-gah-gah," he said.

Mrs. Risley was now able to devote her entire attention to Socks. This remarkable woman, who knew where to find things in a strange house, found Socks's brush in the laundry and went to work brushing him with long, hard strokes. Socks stood with his back braced and his chin raised, luxuriating in the tingle the brush brought to his skin. All the time Mrs. Risley brushed, she talked. "Poor

Skeezix," she said tenderly. "With a baby in the house he feels nobody loves him. Well, Mrs. Risley loves him." With a tip of her finger she rubbed his nose where the hair grew short and flat. How good it felt! "Yes, he is a handsome boy." Socks agreed.

When Mrs. Risley cooked and ate her meat patty, she served Socks a morsel. "Just enough so you won't feel left out," she explained. "We can't let such a handsome boy get fat, can we? No, that wouldn't do at all." Somehow Socks did not mind receiving only one small bite of meat.

By this time Charles William had exhausted the possibilities of Scotch tape and was beginning to be cross with it. He had pulled it from his toe, stuck it to his right hand and then his left, back and forth, and finally succeeded in sticking it to Brown

Bear. He did not want Scotch tape stuck to Brown Bear. Charles William fussed, and Socks looked anxiously to Mrs. Risley.

"Now don't you worry," said Mrs. Risley, pausing to stroke the tabby head. "I'll be right back." Socks was so relaxed that only a moment seemed to go by from the time Charles William was lifted from his playpen until he was smacking away at his bottle in his bedroom crib.

Mrs. Risley pulled a magazine from her survival kit and plumped herself down on the couch where she patted her lap. "*Now,*" she said to Socks, as if this was the moment she had been waiting for.

This was the moment Socks had been waiting for, too. He leaped lightly onto the sitter's lap, which was large, soft, and sweetly perfumed by flower-scented soap. Mrs. Risley possessed the perfect lap, a lap rarely experienced by a cat who lived in a world of people determined to stay thin.

Except for Socks's deep purr of contentment, the room was quiet. In Charles William's room the smacking stopped, but this time Socks had no interest in leftover formula. He no longer had an empty feeling in his

middle. The bottle fell out of the crib with a thump, and the silence that followed meant that Charles William was asleep for the night.

Socks began to knead the perfect lap with his paws, in and out, in and out. His purr deepened, and a dreamy look came into his golden eyes. In and out, in and out. With his eyes half-closed, Socks felt as if he were with his mother and the rest of his litter that he had almost forgotten.

Socks lost all interest in washing. He lay down on the perfect lap and wriggled until he was lying on his back with his four feet in the air and his spine in the trough between Mrs. Risley's plump thighs. Gently and rhythmically she stroked the silky fur on his trusting belly. "Poor old Skeezix," whispered Mrs. Risley, as she stroked Socks's glossy fur. "You were starved for a little love." She turned the pages of her magazine carefully so they would not flick his whiskers and the sound would not disturb him.

Gradually the purrs petered out, and with a final sigh Socks fell into a deep sleep, the first perfect sleep he had enjoyed since Charles William had been carried home from the hospital. Mrs. Risley loved him more than she loved his rival.

Five

A Visit from Nana

A puzzling and, to Socks, inconvenient change took place in the behavior of his mistress. Mrs. Bricker, who usually spent the least possible time housekeeping, now upset the household by a thorough cleaning. Socks had to rewash his paws after he walked across the kitchen floor wet from the mop. The vacuum cleaner drove him from one room to another, and the smell of the ammonia that Mrs. Bricker used to wash the windows drove him out of the house. The only good that came from all this housecleaning was the disappearance of dust from under the bed. Socks could now retreat in safety without sneezing.

Cooking came next. Mrs. Bricker dumped Socks out the back door, so he would not be underfoot. He watched from the windowsill while she made a molded salad, experimented with cake mixes, and tried meat-loaf recipes. Not long afterward, Mr. Bricker, carrying luggage, walked into the house with a thin, brisk woman whom he called Mom but referred to as Nana. Mr. Bricker's mother had arrived to spend her two weeks' vacation visiting her son and his family.

Socks could tell right away that Nana was no Mrs. Risley. He sniffed her luggage for a clue to its contents and then turned his back on all the greetings and washed himself. Exclamations of "Nana's precious is a big boy! Yes, he is!" and "He looks just like his father when he was the same age!" bored Socks. Nana, unlike Mrs. Risley, did not understand the importance of a cat.

After Mr. Bricker's mother had admired her grandson, given the family presents, and been taken on a tour of the house, she said, "Bill, I didn't know you kept a cat." Socks sensed all eyes were on him and looked up from his washing. He saw that Charles William was sitting on his mother's lap staring at his grandmother's shining hair, which was the color of iced tea.

"Good old Socks. He's quite a character,"

said Mr. Bricker. Then to change the subject, he remarked, "What have you done to your hair? It looks different."

"That is between me and my hairdresser." Nana smiled and changed the subject back again. "Are you sure it's a good idea, keeping a cat when there's a baby in the house?"

Mrs. Bricker was quick to defend their pet. "Socks is a clean, healthy cat, and we love him. He's a member of the family."

Socks delicately washed the pink pads on his right front paw.

Nana was not convinced. "Some babies are allergic to cats."

"Not our boy," said Mrs. Bricker. "Charles William hasn't shown any sign of allergy." She took hold of her son's big toe, and said, "He's a big healthy boy. Yes, he is." Charles William, who was drooling because he was teething, looked pleased.

"This little piggy went to market," said Mrs. Bricker, wiggling one rosy toe.

"Ig-gig-gig," said Charles William.

"But aren't you afraid the cat might scratch the baby?" persisted Nana, her glance resting on the frayed corner of the loopy chair where Socks sharpened his claws.

"Not really," said Mrs. Bricker. "I do keep an eye on him when they're in the same room, but he's very patient with Tiffy, the little girl next door. When she picks him up around the middle, he doesn't even struggle. He goes limp until she puts him down, and then he runs away."

"You can't be too careful around a baby." Nana was not persuaded that Socks should remain a member of her son's family.

Socks soon found the grandmother's visit a trial. Everything he did was wrong. When he tried to jump on her lap, his claw snagged her knit dress and he was scolded. Her nylon stockings dancing over the heat vent as they dried in the bathroom were irresistible to him, and he could not understand why she felt he had misbehaved when he pulled them down and played with them. Couldn't she understand that a cat needed to play? When Nana settled on the couch to knit a sweater for her grandson, Socks was so fascinated by the movement of her knitting needles that he had to jump up beside her to watch. She eyed him with disapproval, but when he sat very, very still, the way he sat while watching a bug crawl across the floor, she did not object. He did not take his eyes from those flashing needles until, with one quick swipe of his paw, he reached out and hooked the head of a knitting needle in his claws. The needle slid out of the yarn and flipped to the coffee table with a clatter.

"Now see what you made me do," said Nana crossly. "I just dropped ninety-four stitches." Mrs. Risley would not have spoken to Socks in this tone of voice.

"Isn't it funny the way cats are always attracted to people who don't like them?" said Mrs. Bricker. Socks's feelings were hurt when she picked him up and set him down outside the front door.

As the days passed, Nana grew more critical of Socks. If he scratched, she was sure he was crawling with fleas that might bite Charles William. Every time Socks watched and waited until he could get his paws on Brown Bear, she took it away from him and brushed it off. If her grandson sneezed, she was sure he was allergic to cats. She was constantly brushing cat hair off the couch, and one evening she plucked a cat hair out of her salad. She was polite, though, and did not call attention to it, but the Brickers noticed.

Nights were hardest of all. Because the Brickers' house was small, Nana had to sleep on the couch in the living room while Socks, who considered the couch his bed, was shut in the laundry.

Socks resented this arrangement. Every evening he complained himself hoarse, even though Mr. Bricker interrupted the conversation in the living room to shout, "Socks, be quiet!" Socks lay yowling on the hard floor and groped under the door with his paw. He sat up and threw his shoulder against the door. When nothing, absolutely nothing would free him, his last act before settling

down on the sweat shirt was to plow Kitty
Litter over the floor so someone would have
to sweep it up in the morning.

Socks became so discouraged that each
night he yowled less and sulked more until
one moonlit night when the household had
settled into silence. The laundry was so light
that Socks was restless. He jumped out of his
box, extended his paws as if he were bowing,
enjoyed a good stretch, and then threw his
shoulder against the door, which this time
surprised him by silently opening enough for
a cat to walk through.

Socks was free! He padded through the
kitchen and dining room to the living room,
where Nana was asleep. The pupils of his
eyes widened in the dim light, and as he was
about to spring up on the blanket beside her,
he noticed her suitcase lying open in the

corner of the room. Nana had not understood his curiosity about her luggage and had not allowed him to look inside. Socks trotted across the carpet and after a cautious sniff, stepped into the suitcase. A nylon slip felt smooth to his paw pads and much softer than the old sweat shirt.

Socks was about to use the suitcase for a bed when a ghostly object looming on the desk caught his attention. He stood motionless, staring up at something white gleaming in the darkness. When it did not move and he could not smell it, he sprang to the top of the desk to investigate. There he discovered an astonishing thing: Nana's hair. There in the midst of Mrs. Bricker's books and papers sat the hair on a faceless white head. He had never seen such a sight in his life. His head cocked to one side, Socks patted the soft fibers with a curious paw. He was fascinated. He patted with his other paw. Here was something to play with, and Socks was lonely for play.

With extended claws Socks hooked the hair from the Styrofoam head and batted it over the edge of the desk to the floor. The head rolled over the edge of the desk, too, and landed beside the hair with a soft thump, which made Nana stir in her sleep. Socks sprang on the hair, caught it in his claws, tossed it into the air, and let it fall on the carpet. Then he pounced. He hugged the soft bundle of fibers with his front paws and kicked it with his strong hind feet. He rolled over with the hair still clutched to his body. With his movements muffled by the carpet, he tussled and scuffled and wrestled. He dropped the hair, hid behind a chair, and

pounced again. He pretended to ignore it before he surprised it by catching it in his claws and tossing it into the air.

Finally Socks grew bored with the game. Nana's hair would not fight back. He dropped it in a patch of moonlight and settled for the night on the nylon and lace in Nana's suitcase.

The next morning Socks was awakened by Nana groping for her bedroom slippers. The hair on her head, her second-best hair, was shorter and grayer than the hair on the carpet. Socks yawned so hard that his ears lay back and his pink tongue stretched out of his mouth. He eased his muscles by humping his back like a Halloween cat and leaped onto the carpet, where he proceeded with his morning wash.

"Well!" said Nana in a whisper. "Just what do you think you're doing in here?"

Socks did not care for the tone of her voice. He paused long enough to give her an insolent look, as if to say, "I belong here and you do not," before he continued licking his fur. Soon he turned his head away from Nana to reach the difficult spot behind his shoulder.

Nana, who had not rested well on the lumpy couch, was buttoning her robe when she noticed the naked Styrofoam head on the floor. She was quick to discover her best hair on the carpet. With an angry, *"Oh!"* she snatched it up and stared at it while Socks pretended to ignore her. The Brickers were awake. Water ran in the bathroom, and Mr. Bricker's electric razor buzzed.

"You—you—*cat!*" Nana whispered. "Look what you've done!"

Socks looked, but not for long. Grooming his immaculate white paws was more im-

portant. He found a bit of dried mud between his toes, which needed attention.

Nana examined the netting inside the wig,
and in the desk drawer she found some
Scotch tape, which she used for some hasty
repairs. Then she set what had once been her
best hair on the Styrofoam head and went to
work with her hairbrush. She smoothed and
brushed. She patted and poked. She pinched
waves into place and rolled the ends over her
fingers. When she was sure the bathroom
was free, she picked up the hair and her
clothes and stalked from the living room.

Charles William began to fuss. Socks
was waiting by the refrigerator when Mrs.
Bricker arrived to warm a bottle.

"Out of the way, Socks," said Mrs. Bricker,
giving him a gentle shove with her foot so
she could open the refrigerator door. Socks

meowed and rubbed against her ankles while she set a bottle in a pan of water on the stove.

Mr. Bricker appeared with Charles William, still dressed in sleepers, in his arms.

"Mommy is getting her baby's breakfast just as fast as she can," said Mrs. Bricker in the voice that Socks resented when it was not addressed to him.

Nana joined the family in the kitchen. The sight of her hair silenced her daughter-in-law and made her son stare. Odd little tufts poked out from the once-smooth curls. The silence, broken by the quivery sobs of the hungry baby, was awkward.

"Mom, what happened to your—hair?" asked her son. He did not approve of his mother's wearing a wig. The Brickers thought hair should look natural.

"Nothing," said Nana bravely. "It was

nothing really. Nothing a trip to the hairdresser won't repair."

Mr. Bricker was not satisfied. "Something must have happened to make your hair look like a bird's ne—"

"Bill—" Mrs. Bricker's voice held a warning as Socks purred and rubbed against her legs. He was every bit as hungry as Charles William, but he was much pleasanter.

Nana frowned at Socks in spite of all his charm.

"Socks!" said Mrs. Bricker accusingly. "Did you get into Nana's—hair?"

Attention at last! Socks stood on his hind legs with his front paws braced against Mrs. Bricker and increased the volume of his purr.

"Oh, you bad cat!" Mrs. Bricker unhooked his claws from her housecoat. Charles William drooled and wept. The water on the stove began to bubble and splash over the edge of pan, hissing as it hit the burners. "Now see what you made me do! The bottle is too hot and it takes forever to cool." She removed the pan from the stove and replaced the boiling water with cold water. Socks did not care for the treatment that he was getting. These people were wasting too much time. They neither fed him nor attended to the baby.

"Nana, I'm terribly sorry," said Mrs. Bricker. "I was sure Socks was shut in the laundry. I guess we didn't give the door that little extra shove. If you don't give it that—"

"Now Marilyn, don't worry about a thing," said Nana, determined not to cause trouble. "I'll have my wig washed and set at a beauty shop, and everything will be all right. Now what can I do to help?"

"In a minute you can give Charles William his cereal." Mrs. Bricker tripped over Socks on her way to the cupboard for a custard cup. "Everything is so hectic because we forgot to set the alarm—"

Socks had endured too much delay from these chattering people. Charm had not worked. His patience was at an end. He nipped at Mrs. Bricker's ankle to remind her that he wanted his breakfast and he wanted it now. Two tiny drops of blood appeared on her bare leg.

"Marilyn! That cat bit you!" Nana was shocked. "You're bleeding!"

"Socks!" Mr. Bricker shouted in such a terrible voice that Socks was stunned. Never had his master spoken to him that way. He cringed against a cupboard and looked up at Mr. Bricker with wide, frightened eyes.

A fussy, teething baby, a husband in a hurry to leave for his classes and his job in the University library, the strain of a mother-in-law in a house too small for guests, papers waiting to be typed, and a nipping cat were all too much for Mrs. Bricker. "Bill, get that cat out of here," she said with tears in her voice. "*Please* get that cat out of here before I go out of my mind."

To his astonishment, Socks, who had not meant to hurt Mrs. Bricker, found himself lifted and dumped out the back door without so much as a kind word or a bite of breakfast. He stood lashing his tail in anger, and in a few minutes when he began to understand that no one was going to let him in, he jumped to the sill of the dining-room window where he could see Nana holding Charles William and spooning cereal into his mouth. Mrs. Bricker, with a Band-Aid on her ankle, was dropping bread into a toaster, and Mr. Bricker was pouring cereal from a box. Socks meowed peevishly to let his owners

know he was cross, hungry, and unfairly treated.

"Beat it, you cat," said Mr. Bricker, as he reached for a carton of half-and-half. "We can't have a cat that bites in *this* house."

"Oy-doy-doy!" shouted Charles William, happy to be eating breakfast at last and secure in the love of his family.

SIX

Old Taylor

"Don't you like Socks anymore?" Tiffy asked Mr. Bricker, who was trying to spade a section of the backyard while Socks rolled in the dirt at his feet. The Brickers planned to make a vegetable garden, so Charles William could have nice fresh vegetables to eat.

"Sure we like him, Tiffy," said Mr. Bricker.

"Then how come he sleeps in the garage?" persisted Tiffy.

"We can't have a cat that bites in the house with a baby," Mr. Bricker explained.

"He doesn't bite me. He could sleep at my home if he wanted." Tiffy looked wistfully at Socks squirming in the dirt. He would have to spend the rest of the afternoon grooming himself, a small price to pay for a good roll that satisfied all the places he wanted scratched and made his skin tingle. He missed the sort of brushing Mrs. Risley had given him, but the sitter never came again. The young couple could not afford her.

Tiffy squatted beside Socks. "Do you want to come and live at my house?" she asked.

Socks, who had finished rolling in the dirt, sat up and, after considering Tiffy a moment, allowed her to pet him. Since he had become an outdoor cat, he was grateful for attention from anyone, even Tiffy, and the two had formed a cautious friendship.

"See!" said Tiffy to Mr. Bricker. "Socks likes me. He wants to live at my house." She made the mistake of patting his head, and Socks moved away. Petting and patting were not the same. He was disappointed in her.

"A cat's heart is where his dish is," said Mr. Bricker.

Mr. Bricker was wrong. Socks's dish and water bowl had been moved to the back step, and his bed had been moved to the garage, where a window was left open so he could come and go. Still, his heart remained in the house with his family. Loneliness and curiosity drove Socks to spend more and more time sitting on the windowsill watching all that went on inside. He watched Mr. Bricker

shadowbox in front of the playpen and listened to Charles William laugh. He watched
Charles William grab Brown Bear by one leg
and beat him against the playpen pad, and
he heard him shout, "Id-did-did!" He was
curious for a closer look at the plastic ball
filled with water and sloshing plastic fish. He
saw Charles William support himself on his
hands and knees and crawl across the pen.
He watched him grab the bars and pull himself unsteadily to his feet.

"See the kitty," said Mrs. Bricker many

times a day, as she looked up from her typewriter. "The kitty is looking at you." Charles
William paused in throwing his toys outside
his playpen or pounding on a pie tin to stare
at Socks. Sometimes he watched Socks without his mother telling him to.

Loneliness was not the only trouble in
Socks's new life. Jays scattered his dry food
and swooped at him whenever they came to
steal. He felt threatened on Tuesday morn-
ings when the garbage men came, and he
was afraid of the milkman. But his biggest
worry was Old Taylor, the black cat with
the torn ear and bulging jowls, who lived
across the back fence and belonged to a family named Taylor.

Although the fence was the property of
the house rented by the Brickers and should
have been part of Socks's territory, Old Tay-

lor made it his own by sleeping on it whenever the sun was out. This habit annoyed Socks, who sometimes wanted to sit on the fence out of Tiffy's reach when he grew bored with her attention. However, the two cats had come to an understanding. Old Taylor would beat up Socks if Socks tried to sit on the fence while Old Taylor was using it.

One morning Socks, who had fallen asleep on the warm hood of the old station wagon, was awakened by the sound of a late spring rain driving against the garage. The car hood had grown cold and hard. After a bow, a stretch, and a brief wash, Socks sprang to the windowsill, where he saw that the neighborhood was still dark. There was no hope of breakfast, but he might find dry food left in his dish from the night before. The grass was cold and wet to his paws as he ran through the downpour in the direction of the back step.

In the dim light Socks saw a sinister black shape crouched at his dish in the dry spot below the eaves. Old Taylor! Through the sound of rainwater gurgling in the drainpipe, Socks heard the crunch of teeth crushing dry cat food. This intrusion would not do at all. Old Taylor had his side of the fence, and Socks had his. Socks would not quibble about the fence itself, but his food was a different matter. He crouched, flattened his ears and hissed, hoping to frighten the other cat, but prepared to defend his dish if he must.

Old Taylor merely glanced in his direction and went on gnashing and crunching. Socks's honor as a cat could not excuse such

rudeness. He advanced, still hissing, through the rain. Old Taylor stopped gnawing and grinding. He flattened his ears and hissed back from the dry spot on the step.

By now Socks was not only angry, he was soaking wet. He ignored the rain and continued to crouch, changing his hiss to a light singsong wail intended to warn Old Taylor that he meant what he said. His tune did not frighten Old Taylor. The black cat returned

the sound louder and meaner. No young up-
start was going to tell him anything. The fur
of the two cats rose along their spines. They
wailed and howled and caterwauled, and all
during the eerie duet they were moving
closer to one another with their fangs bared
and their ears laid back.

Nose to nose, Socks found Old Taylor a
terrifying sight with his ear torn and his fur
standing out on his great black jowls. But

Socks did not back down. Finally, with a terrible scream, the cats were on one another, a growling, snarling, yowling tangle. They clawed and bit and tumbled down the steps into a puddle. They rolled across the soaking grass and into freshly spaded earth. They floundered and wallowed in the mud. Old Taylor was on his back, thrashing at Socks with punishing blows of his strong hind feet. Socks felt claws and teeth through his fur. He hurt, he was bleeding, and Old Taylor had sprayed him. The black cat was too much for him.

Socks no longer cared about his dry food. Let the old tomcat have it. Socks wanted to get away, to untangle himself from the snarling, biting mass of muddy black fur. Somehow he did get away and ran for the garage while Old Taylor sent singsong warnings

after him through the downpour. When
Socks tried to leap to the windowsill, the
weight of the mud on his fur made him fall.
When he tried to lick his bleeding forepaw,
the rasps on his tongue scraped up a mouth-
ful of mud. Cold, wet, stiff with mud and in
pain, Socks needed help.

Lights were coming on in the bedrooms,
bathrooms, and kitchens of the neighborhood. Old Taylor had disappeared. Slowly
and painfully Socks made his way through
the rain, through the scattered cat food, now
soggy and unappetizing, to his own back
door where he cried a small, desperate meow
for help.

Mrs. Bricker, who was in the kitchen,
heard and must have understood, for she im-
mediately opened the back door. "Socks!"
she cried, shocked.

Socks looked up at her with sad, defeated eyes.

"Oh, poor Socks!" Mrs. Bricker opened the door wider, and Socks stepped painfully into the laundry. "Bill! Come and look at Socks. He's been in a fight!"

Mr. Bricker came down the hall with his bathrobe flying. "Why you poor old fellow," he said, when he saw his cat.

Socks waited helplessly.

"And he's *bleeding!*" cried Mrs. Bricker. "What'll we do? He can't lick all that mud."

Mr. Bricker agreed. "And if we tried to give him a bath, he'd climb the wall."

"We can't let the mud dry," said Mrs. Bricker. "Adobe bricks are made out of mud like this. If it dries, he'll turn into an adobe cat."

"Try wet bath towels." Mr. Bricker

snatched a clean towel from the tangle on top of the dryer and dampened it under the kitchen faucet. Mrs. Bricker did the same. They knelt and began to rub Socks. How good the warm towels and gentle hands felt.

Charles William awoke and fussed in his crib, but this time Socks got the attention, which made him feel better.

"Poor Socks," grieved Mrs. Bricker, as she swabbed with a second towel and then a third. "It's all our fault for shutting you out." She dropped the towel into the washing machine and reached for a clean diaper.

"Socks should learn to roll over on his back and kick with his hind feet when he gets in a fight," said Mr. Bricker, who was interested in all sports. "His strength is in his hind legs. He should hang on with his front paws and give Old Taylor everything he's got with his hind legs."

"Bill, you can't coach a cat." Mrs. Bricker laughed affectionately as she held another diaper under the kitchen faucet.

Charles William increased the volume of his fussing and began to rock his crib.

"Socks needs us," his mother called to him. "You'll have to wait." Then she said to her husband, "Bill, can't we let Socks live in the house again? I know he didn't mean to bite so hard that time, and I always watch him when he's in the room with Charles William."

"I don't see why not," said Mr. Bricker, scrubbing the matted fur with a clean diaper. "He's older and wiser now, but we'll still have to keep an eye on him."

Charles William began to bump his crib against the wall.

"I'm coming, I'm coming." Mrs. Bricker rinsed her hands in the kitchen and, without bothering to change him, carried Charles William to his high chair, which she turned so that he could watch from the kitchen. She handed him a spoon to bang and went back to swabbing Socks.

Charles William enthusiastically whacked

the spoon on the tray of his high chair until Socks caught his interest. He stopped whacking to stare. He had never seen a mud-covered cat before, and he had to give the matter some thought. "Ticky?" he said at last. "Ticky?"

Socks understood that Charles Williams was talking to him, and beneath his misery he felt the beginning of a new interest in the baby.

Both parents stopped scrubbing the cat to look at their son and then at one another. "Did you hear that?" cried the mother. "He's talking! He's trying to say *kitty*!"

"Smart boy!" said the proud father.

Socks was forgotten. Charles William had spoken a word—well, almost. Ticky! Imagine that. Charles William had called Socks Ticky. His mother would write his first word in his baby book. His father would write the news to Nana, maybe even phone collect. Charles William, overwhelmed with his own cleverness, heaved the spoon across the kitchen.

Then the Brickers noticed the clock. If they did not hurry, Mr. Bricker would be late for class. He rushed off to dress while Mrs. Bricker dashed about the kitchen, trying to prepare one breakfast for the parents and another for the baby.

"Ticky?" said Charles William, pleased with himself and eager to rekindle the excitement that he had caused.

"That's right," answered his proud mother. "We can't forget Ticky." She returned to the laundry, where Socks was licking his wound, and offered him a piece of meat with her fingers. He was sorry that he had no appetite.

Mrs. Bricker turned on the clothes dryer

to warm the laundry and closed the door. This time Socks did not object to being shut in. He crouched on aching joints and, allowing for the weight of mud on his fur, leaped to the top of the dryer, where he settled himself to lick his bleeding leg in the tangle of clean diapers waiting to be folded.

In the kitchen Charles William demanded admiration. "Ticky?" he said, slapping his palms on the tray of his high chair. "Ticky?"

"Kit-tee," said Mrs. Bricker.

"Ticky," said Charles William, and laughed. He had invented a game.

Socks was soothed by the hum of the dryer and by the heat rising through the diapers. His throat began to vibrate with a hoarse and rusty-sounding purr, as if he had not purred for a long, long time. "Kit-tee." "Ticky." Mrs. Bricker and the baby were talking about him.

seven
Socks and Charles William

Socks soon discovered, once his bed and dish had been returned to their old place in the laundry, that being inside the house with Charles William was quite different from watching him through the window. Charles William had outgrown his morning nap, and whenever Socks was in the room, he no longer was content to stay in his pen playing with Brown Bear or with his plastic ball filled with sloshing plastic fish. The minute his mother set him down inside the pen he began to fuss. If his mother ignored his fussing, he clung to the bars and howled. His playpen bored him, and he wanted out. If the cat was out, he should be out, too.

All this howling and shaking of wooden bars worried Socks, who sat beside the playpen like the Sphinx, with his paws flat in front, staring at the only human being he knew who was anywhere near his own size. The louder Charles William cried, the more uneasy Socks became until finally he ran meowing to Mrs. Bricker to tell her that she must do something to stop the crying.

Mrs. Bricker always relented. "All right, you two," she said, as she lifted her son out of the pen and set him on the carpet. "You win." She was careful never to have Socks and the baby alone when Charles William was outside his playpen.

Charles William was into everything. He tried to chew the lamp cord until his mother came running to pry it out of his fingers and to unplug the lamp. He crawled into the laundry and threw Socks's dry food all over the floor. Mrs. Bricker started serving Socks's meals on top of the clothes dryer.

Charles William pulled magazines off the coffee table with a slam that woke Socks with a start. He cried when his mother would not let him taste the dead moths he found. He sat in his high chair yelling "oy-doy-doy" into his cup, because he could make more noise that way. He stuffed his mouth with cottage cheese and blew it all over the kitchen for his mother to wipe up. He pulled pans out of the cupboards and banged them on the floor, a sound most disturbing to a cat's sensitive ears. When given an educational·toy, three wooden rings to fit on a peg, he threw away the rings, grabbed the peg as if it were a tomahawk, and pounded the floor with its base.

Most of all Charles William delighted in crawling after Socks. "Ticky?" he said hopefully. "Ticky?"

Socks came to accept his new name from the baby. Let the Brickers call him Ticky, and all they earned was a look of contempt.

"Pet the kitty gently," said Mrs. Bricker, when Charles William reached for Socks's tail.

Socks learned to put up with Charles William and, when necessary, to escape

under the dining-room table where he was
fenced in by chair legs.

"See, the kitty's tired," said Mrs. Bricker
to Charles William, when Socks had fled to
safety. Actually Mrs. Bricker was the one
who was tired.

Charles William was not only an active
baby, he was growing heavier, and lifting
him in and out of his high chair or onto the
table in his room, where his diapers were
changed, was tiring to his mother. In the

afternoon, after she put Charles William down in his crib with his bottle and Brown Bear for his nap, Mrs. Bricker kicked off her sandals and fell asleep on the couch in the living room.

There was nothing Socks enjoyed so much as a warm body to lean against while he washed, but as soon as he settled himself against Mrs. Bricker and was grooming himself with long, hard licks, pausing to chew the rough spots, she pushed him to the floor. "Socks, *please*," she said. "Be a good cat."

In a moment Socks was back against the exhausted mother, licking, chewing, and occasionally scratching until his fur was sleek and his paws snowy. Mrs. Bricker, who knew when she was defeated and was too tired to protest, slept, and after a few minutes of vibrant purring so did Socks.

One afternoon, when Mrs. Bricker had put Charles William in his crib for his nap, Socks jumped down from the top of the clothes dryer, where he had been crunching dry cat food. He was passing the baby's room on his way to join Mrs. Bricker on the couch as Charles William heaved his bottle out of his crib. The top, which he had managed to twist, came off, and the sight of all the milk spilling across the floor caught Socks's attention.

Socks went to investigate, and although the milk was ordinary milk instead of the formula he once had enjoyed, he crouched and lapped while Charles William watched. When Socks had finished and was tidying his whiskers, Charles William got on his hands and knees and began to rock his crib as if he wanted to show what he could do.

The crib began to move. Charles William rocked harder. The crib slid across the bare floor to the door, which Charles William was able to reach out to and push shut, an accomplishment that pleased him. He rocked some more, past the door, until the crib touched the wall and barred the door.

Socks looked up at Charles William and meowed. How was he going to get out with the door shut?

Charles William was delighted to have the cat speak to him personally. This was something new. Socks meowed again. He did not want to be shut in the bedroom when he was supposed to be napping in the living room.

Charles William wanted to amuse the cat. He worked at a crack in his plastic-covered crib bumper, tearing at it until he pulled out a tuft of cotton, which he threw out between the bars of his crib.

With alert eyes Socks watched the fluff floating toward the floor. A second fluff followed, and a third. Socks leaped to clap it between his paws as if it were a butterfly. The baby chortled and tossed out a bigger piece of cotton. Socks leaped for that one, too, dropped it, and batted it across the floor. Now the crack in the plastic was big enough so that Charles William could get both his small hands into it. He pulled out gob after gob of cotton for the cat's amusement.

Socks leaped and pounced and raced in a wild ballet, skidding through what was left of the milk, rolling over with cotton in his paws, while Charles William laughed and pulled out more cotton. Socks leaped for that, too, pleased to play with the fluffy stuff, pleased to entertain an admiring audience. Faster and faster Socks raced and leaped. Charles William screamed with laughter. Socks heard the padding sound of Mrs. Bricker hurrying down the hall in her bare feet, but he paid no attention.

Charles William was silent when he heard the doorknob turn, and Socks paused to pant. Mrs. Bricker tried to open the door, but she could not because of the crib wedged in the corner. "Oh!" she cried, and rattled the door. "Charles William, are you all right?" she asked, as if she expected him to answer. Then, after a pause, she added, "Socks! Are you in there?"

Charles William's attention returned to the torn crib bumper. On with the game! Handfuls of cotton snowed down from the crib for Socks, and Charles William laughed harder than he had ever laughed in all his ten months.

The door rattled again. "Charles William, what are you doing?" Mrs. Bricker's voice was frightened.

His mother could not get in! Charles William found this development so funny that he laughed even harder. He stuck out his tongue and blew. *Thith-puth-putt.* He found his new noise hilarious.

"What am I going to do?" Mrs. Bricker asked herself, and ran down the hall in her bare feet. In a moment Socks heard her running out the back door, and in another moment he saw her anxious face above the windowsill.

Charles William pulled out the last handful of cotton and threw it to Socks. His mother was outside, and he and the cat were

inside. Charles William thought this situation was a huge joke.

Socks was tired of chasing cotton. He lay on his side panting while Mrs. Bricker pushed at the window.

Charles William did not want the fun to end. He was even willing to sacrifice Brown Bear by throwing him over the crib railing. Socks got to his feet, waggled his rump, and sprang on the bear.

"Socks!" shouted Mrs. Bricker through the closed window. "You stop that!" No matter how hard she pounded on the frame she still could not budge the window, which was too high for her.

Socks saw no need to obey. There was nothing she could do to stop his sparring with Brown Bear.

Charles William threw his blanket out of the crib and looked around for something else to amuse the cat. His sharp eyes saw a tiny tear in the wallpaper beside the door-jamb. He grasped the bit of paper and pulled.

"No, no!" shouted his mother, who had papered that room herself to get it ready for her new baby. "Charles William, no, no!"

Thith-puth-putt. Charles William blew again. He did not have to mind his mother. He pulled off a long, satisfying shred of blue paper printed with yellow daisies. All by himself, he pulled it off! Nobody helped him. Delighted with his skill and cleverness, he dropped the curl of paper through the bars of his crib to share with Socks. He laughed so hard that he began to hiccough.

"Oh dear," said Mrs. Bricker. "Charles William, be a good boy while I run and get a stepladder."

Charles William sat hiccoughing while

Socks sparred with Brown Bear, and then he noticed the light switch beside the door. Still hiccoughing, he pulled himself to his feet and worked at the switch until he found the secret of flipping it. The ceiling light went on. Charles William actually turned on the light all by himself! He had flipped the switch by the door, and the light had gone on up there. He had turned on the light just like a grownup. He turned it off. Miraculous! On. Even more miraculous. Off. On. Off. On.

The fun, the laughter and hiccoughs, and the magic were suddenly too much for the baby. Charles William sat down with a thump and lay back with his thumb in his mouth. Gradually his hiccoughs subsided.

Socks, who had been distracted from Brown Bear by the light, lay panting in the midst of the cotton. Only half-sorry that the fun had ended, he was pleased that Charles William was learning to play. He looked up at the baby and, after a moment of hesitation, leaped lightly to the top of the chest of drawers and from there into the crib.

Charles William smiled drowsily around the thumb in his mouth. This had been the best afternoon of his whole life, the most interesting, the most exciting, the most fun. He had found someone to play with.

Socks turned around until he found exactly the right spot beside Charles William. He lay down with his back pressed against the back of the baby whose thumb dropped out of his mouth as he fell asleep.

Socks licked a paw, rubbed an ear, and let his washing go at that. For the first time since he had slept on Mrs. Risley's lap, he was completely at peace. The crib was com-

fortable, the room quiet. The rustle of
Charles William's plastic pants inside his
corduroy overalls was friendly and soothing.
Socks now had a playmate and companion.
He rested his chin on his outstretched fore-
leg, but before he could sleep the stepladder
bumping against the house made him raise
his head.

Socks heard Tiffy say, "Mrs. Bricker, why
are you climbing the ladder?"

"Because Charles William locked me out
of the bedroom," answered Mrs. Bricker.

"I didn't know he was big enough," said
Tiffy.

"It's a long story," said Mrs. Bricker. "I'll
tell you later."

Socks watched Mrs. Bricker raise the
window and throw her leg over the sill. She
paused when she saw him so close to her

baby. Socks gazed at her with a long, clear look that told her plainly, I have found a friend. This is where I belong.

Socks did not take his eyes from Charles William's mother, and she did not take her eyes from him as she climbed into the room and slid the crib away from the door. Then they both noticed Tiffy watching through the window.

"Tiffy, go back!" ordered Mrs. Bricker in a loud whisper. "You might fall."

"Lucky Charles William," said Tiffy, before she disappeared from the window.

Socks returned his gaze to Mrs. Bricker, who picked up Brown Bear and set him in the crib. With a smile, she reached over to stroke Socks's fur, giving him permission to stay with Charles William.

Only then did Socks close his eyes.